Time to go to sleep!

Early Bird got into bed.

Wiggly Worm went to bed

in the flowerpot!

Good night, Wiggly Worm!

Good night, Early Bird!

Early Bird took his bath
with a sailboat.
Wiggly Worm took his
bath with his hat on.

Daddy gave Early Bird
and Wiggly Worm
a piggyback ride upstairs.

cuckoo!

Wiggly Worm ate
a lot of peas.

They had a good supper.

"Come with me,"
said Early Bird.
All the way home,
Wiggly Worm
and Early Bird
played jump-worm.

The sun was going down.
Early Bird
had to hurry home
for supper.

"That's right,"
said the fellow.
"My name is
Wiggly Worm."

Pppppop!

"Why, it's you!"

said Early Bird.

But the worm was stuck
in his hole.

"Give a <u>big</u> pull,
Early Bird!"

Early Bird took the worm
in his beak and pulled.

"Don't cry,"
said the fellow.
"There's a worm
right over there.
Just hop over
and pull him out."

Early Bird began to cry.

"What's the matter?"
said a funny fellow.

"I can't find a worm,"
said Early Bird.

"You mean,
'Hello, mouse tail'!"
said Freddie Field Mouse.

Then he scampered
back into his hole.

In the garden
Early Bird saw
a wiggly thing.

"Hello, worm,"
Early Bird said.

"I am <u>not</u> a worm!"

said Bunny Rabbit.

"Worms wiggle all over.

Go look in the garden."

Early Bird

saw something

in the ground.

"Are you a worm?"

asked Early Bird.

"Are you a worm?"
asked Early Bird.

"No, I am a frog,"
said a fat fellow on a log.
"Worms live in holes."

"Are you a worm?"
asked Early Bird.
"No," said a bug
on a flower.
"I am a ladybug."

"A worm wiggles.
It lives in a hole
in the ground,"
said Mommy Bird.

So Early Bird went out
to find a worm.

"Why don't you find a worm
to play with?"
Mommy Bird said.
"What is a worm?"
asked Early Bird.

Look at what
Early Bird
ate for breakfast!

Then he put on

his blue sailor suit.

Early Bird
brushed his beak and
combed his feathers.

He went to the bathroom
and washed his face.

The sun
was shining.

Early Bird hopped
out of bed.

Richard Scarry's
The Early Bird

BEGINNER BOOKS
A Division of Random House, Inc.
Random House 🏠 New York

Grolier Books is a division of Grolier Enterprises, Inc.

Library of Congress Cataloging-in-Publication Data
Scarry, Richard. The early bird / by Richard Scarry.
  p. cm. — (Step into reading. A step 1 book)
"Adapted from The early bird, 1968 by Richard Scarry."
SUMMARY: After several cases of mistaken identity Early Bird finally finds a
worm to play with. ISBN 0-679-88920-5 (pbk.) — 0-679-98920-X (lib. bdg.)
[1. Birds—Fiction.   2. Worms—Fiction.   3. Animals—Fiction.]
I. Title. II. Series: Step into Reading.
Step 1 book.   PZ7.S327Ear   1999   [E]—dc21   98-28180

Printed in the United States of America 10 9 8 7 6 5 4 3 2 1

GROLIER
B O O K S

Richard Scarry's
The Early Bird